Cliff Edge

by

Jane A. C. West

Illustrated by Stephen Elford

For Paul Ainsworth – climbing guru

With special thanks to:

Ann Bailey
Bethany
Megan Broadhead
Freya
Harry
Jack
Tremere Lindo
Martin
Lynn Noble
Sam Straw

First published in 2009 in Great Britain by
Barrington Stoke Ltd
18 Walker St, Edinburgh, EH3 7LP

www.barringtonstoke.co.uk

ISBN: 978-1-84299-610-2

Printed in Great Britain by Bell & Bain Ltd

Contents

Chapter 1
Freaks

Another van full of freaks drove into the small town of Oakhurst. Danny felt envy for their easy life. No school, no work and no family. They just did what they wanted.

Oakhurst was a small, American, one-horse town on the edge of California's huge Yosemite National Park.

Danny's friend, Cristo, joked that Oakhurst was such a boring one-horse town that even the one horse had left.

Oakhurst was in the middle of nowhere – but there were two things that the people had a lot of, time and mountains. Everyone was into climbing – there was nothing else to do, except get drunk or sniff petrol.

Most of the shops sold climbing gear, ropes, boots, and the thin slipper-type rock shoes that hard-core climbers used. Climbers like Danny and the rock rat freaks.

The real name for 'freaks' was 'free climbers'. They were guys – and some girls – who liked to climb alone. They'd run up rock faces like so many spiders. Then they used their ropes to get down. This was abseiling.

They lived for climbing. Nothing else mattered. They slept in their vans, worked only when they needed money for food and left at the end of the summer. Danny didn't know where they went. Did they go back to a normal life?

There was another group of free climbers who went solo. This meant they climbed without ropes. No ropes, no safety gear – and death if you took a wrong step.

Danny thought that the free solo guys were crazy. He liked climbing, but free solo was like the circus with no safety net – and death or glory as the prize.

"It's the rush," said one of them to Danny. "There's nothing like it. It's just you and the rock face. It's the only time you're really free."

Danny shook his head. But it was hard not to listen to the part of him that said, *What could be a bigger thrill than risking it all? Risking your life?* Danny was a good climber, but it was stupid to climb without ropes. Wasn't it?

"It's a one-way ticket, Danny," said Cristo. "One day that guy will fall and he'll be crippled or dead. Only idiots climb free solo. If you want a long and happy life don't even think about joining them – they've got a death wish."

"I'm not that mad!" grinned Danny. "Nothing on earth would make me free solo. Nothing."

But Fate was listening ... and Fate had a plan.

Chapter 2
Dogwood Trail

The summer heat had turned the grass to dust – even the air was burning hot.

"Let's go camping," said Cristo. "It'll be cooler in the mountains. We could hike out to the Falls and climb El Cap. Then we can go over to Glacier Point and stay for a few

days. We'll relax, swim in the river and
chill. Maybe climb the Dome."

"Nah, the Dome's too easy but let's do
El Cap. See if we can beat the record of
climbing it in 2 hours and 45 minutes," said
Danny.

"Dream on, my friend. Dream on."

That night they put up their tents. The sweet smell from the flowers of the dogwood trees filled the air.

Danny and Cristo made a fire and counted the stars.

"I like it here," said Cristo. "It's so still."

Danny nodded. "Yeah. It's real."

It was one of those times when good friends didn't have to speak.

The next day the boys got their gear ready. They took food, water, a tent, sleeping bags, a compass, ropes, hiking boots and rock shoes.

This was their plan. They would hike to the waterfall, camp by the river and then climb the huge rock mountain of El Cap. They could forget that they had parents and school to go back to.

They had both hiked in the mountains before and knew what to do. They had told their parents where they would be camping and they had taken mobile phones. There weren't many places you could get a good signal, but it made their parents happy. And you never knew when a mobile would come in handy in the mountains.

Chapter 3
El Cap

Danny and Cristo walked past the Falls. The winter snow was long gone and the famous waterfall was dry.

On the other side of the valley lay the huge rock tower called El Cap. It was 1,000 metres of steep cliff face. It was hard. It was cruel.

There were two ways to climb El Cap, the south-west path and the south-east path. Not that most people would call these 'paths'. They were scary death-trails. Both were very hard. Only really good climbers risked them.

There was a third way up the mountain. Between the two safer paths was a sharp point of rock. It was called 'The Nose' because of its shape.

It took most normal people two days to climb 'The Nose'. The all time record was 2 hours and 45 minutes. Climbing 'The Nose' gave you a rush. The climber who did it would be a hero. But you had to be a bit crazy. Or very crazy.

Early in the morning the huge stone mountain glowed red and orange in the rising sun.

"Today's the day," said Cristo. "We're going to free climb El Cap!"

The boys checked and re-checked their gear. You didn't mess with El Cap. Everything had to be perfect.

They had an easy hike across the valley then gazed up at the mountain. They were going to take the south-west path.

Danny shivered even though the sun was warm.

"Man!" said Cristo. "El Cap is a monster. Let's go!"

Danny took in a great gulp of air and started to climb. His rock shoes gripped the stone surface and his fingers found cracks where he could pull himself up. He could see Cristo to his left but they didn't speak. Free climbing was all about silence. The climb was just you and the rock face. You shared it later.

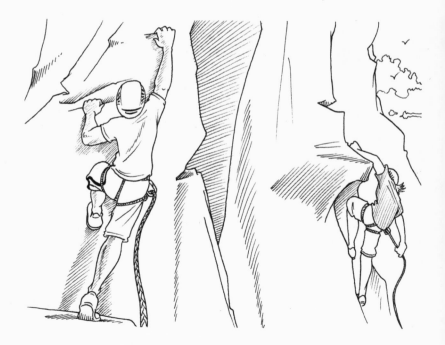

Danny started to think. *What would it be like to climb El Cap solo – without ropes. Would it be so bad?* He'd climbed this far without needing a rope – but he still wore one for safety.

He put it out of his mind. Climbing was about control – not risk.

They climbed in silence, without stopping, for two hours. They were over half way up the south-west path. They had made good time. They saw no one. They seemed alone on the mountain.

"Hey, Danny!" yelled Cristo. "Let's take a photo – so we can show off to the girls at school next year."

"Let's get up to that ledge first," said Danny. "It's safer."

"Nah, man! It's a better shot here," said Cristo.

He felt around in his back-pack to get out his camera phone. He leaned back on his rope to get a better view.

"Watch it, Cristo," said Danny.

"One for the girls!" said Cristo, grinning.

In that second, Cristo's feet slipped on the smooth rock. He gave a yell, dropped the camera phone and fell.

"Cristo! Cristo!" shouted Danny.

There was no sound.

Cristo had fallen 30 metres. His rope
had stopped him from crashing to his death.

Danny could see his friend dangling below on the end of his rope.

"Cristo?" Danny called again.

There was no reply.

As fast as he dared, Danny let himself down the rock face to get to his friend. His rock shoes sent a shower of small stones racing down the mountain. Danny could hear them bouncing off Cristo's helmet.

Danny swore loudly. He could see blood on Cristo's face. His eyes were shut. He was out cold. That wasn't all, Danny could see that Cristo's left arm was hanging at an odd angle. The arm was broken. Cristo could never finish the climb like that. He needed help. Fast.

Chapter 4
Free Solo

Danny had to get help. He felt into his pocket for his phone. It wasn't there. He tried his other pockets. Nothing there. This was bad. He must have left his phone at the campsite. Cristo's phone was hundreds of metres below – smashed on the rocks.

Danny had to choose. He could stay and hope for help from passing climbers – or he could go and get help.

Lots of people climbed El Cap, but today Danny hadn't seen anyone on the south-west path. If he did nothing, they might have to wait for days before help came. There was no way Danny could lower Cristo down on a

rope. He was too heavy and it was too risky.
Danny could end up killing them both. The
only thing to do was to leave Cristo and go
for help.

He hated to think of Cristo waking up
alone and in pain. But sometimes Fate
makes you take the hard path.

"Hang in there, Cristo, I'm going for
help," he said.

Danny knew that this was Cristo's best chance – his only chance – of staying alive. He made sure that the knots on Cristo's ropes were firm, keeping him safe as he hung on the cliff edge. Cristo could not live through the night on El Cap with a broken arm. The night air would be very cold – below freezing – and Cristo would be in shock from the pain in his smashed arm.

Danny had to get help as fast as he could. To do this he needed to get over to the easier south-east path. It was where most people climbed. Someone there was sure to have a phone. But to get there Danny had to cross over 'The Nose'. He tried not to think of the danger in doing that.

Danny made up his mind fast. Cristo didn't have much time before he went into shock.

"Damn ropes!" said Danny. "I'll be better off without them."

And in that moment he knew what he had to do.

"I'll climb free solo. It'll be faster."

He unhooked himself from his ropes and took a breath. Far, far below him, the river shone like a tiny ribbon of silver.

His fingers found cracks in the rock to cling to. His rock shoes found a small bump in the smooth stone to grip. Danny started moving across the rock face like a spider. Up and up.

Soon his hands were sore and his legs hurt badly. He kept going.

Twice he cut his arms on sharp rocks. The sweat poured into his eyes, making them sting. He kept going.

Rocks fell from above and grazed his back and shoulders. He kept going.

Danny was panting so hard that his chest burned. But just thinking about Cristo kept him going. "I won't let you die, Cristo," he said. "I won't." He gritted his teeth and climbed on.

At last, Danny was at the point of rock called 'The Nose'. He held on with a tight grip, his teeth clenched and his eyes shut. His cheek was pressed against the cold cliff face. He reached out his arm slowly – trying to find a finger hold. The rock felt smooth. He felt around. Nothing.

Danny began to feel panic rising in waves. "Must stay calm," he said. "Must stay calm."

His fingers found a tiny crack in the rock. He grabbed hold and swung his body forward. With his free hand he felt around for something to hold on to. He hung for a second by the finger-tips of one hand. His whole body was held there by just those four fingers. The sweat on his hands made it hard to get a firm grip. He could feel his hold slipping.

In a panic, Danny clawed at the rock.
His torn nails left red streaks of blood on
the cliff.

But Fate would not let him die. Not yet.

His feet found a 2cm ledge and he clung
on. His whole body was shaking. His heart
was pounding like a road drill.

Chapter 5
Free Fall

Danny could see the gentle slope of the south-east path. So near – but so far. He closed his eyes and prayed. "Lord, I need some help."

He forced himself to relax. He tried to empty his mind and focus on the climb.

He took some deep breaths. His heart rate slowed and his mind became as clear as ice water. He moved smoothly across the rock face, as easily as if he were crossing the road.

A huge stone stuck out, blocking his path. It was the rock that climbers called 'The Great Roof' and it was in Danny's way.

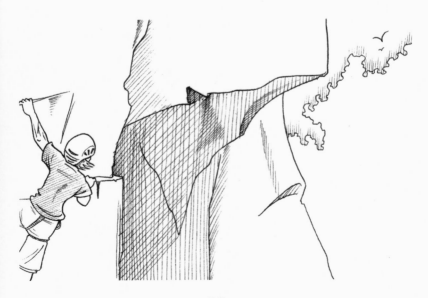

With great care, he took the spare rope from round his waist. A metal hook had been left by climbers in the cliff face. Danny didn't know how long it had been there, or if it could take the full load of his body. But there was no going back.

He pushed the rope through the hook,
then checked the knots around his waist.

He looked down, then jumped.

For a moment it felt as if he was falling.
But the hook held firm. Danny swung like a
child on a swing, higher and higher. The
rusty hook started to bend. Danny swung
once more, pushing himself up and over the
rock shelf. The old hook gave way and broke

in half. But it had done its job. Danny had
made it.

He fell to his knees, happy to be on firm
ground again.

A party of climbers rushed up to him. They hadn't been able to see him until now, because the rock shelf had blocked their view. If Danny had known that they were there, he could have asked them to pull him up. He would not have had to risk his life.

"Wow! That was amazing!" they said. "Did you just free climb 'The Nose'? No way! You even did a free solo on some of it! No one as young as you has ever done that before! It took us four days to climb up here. Are you crazy?"

Danny sat down. Still out of breath, he gasped out his story. He was so worn out and still so afraid, that he was shaking. One of the climbers saw that Danny wasn't just a kid on a dare, something bad had happened. The climber phoned for the rescue helicopter on his mobile.

Chapter 6
End Game

Two weeks later, Danny and Cristo were sitting under a Dogwood tree sharing a can of coke. Cristo had seven stitches in his head and his arm was in a sling. He'd broken it in three places and badly hurt his shoulder. At first the doctors said they couldn't save his arm, but they'd done it.

"The doctors say I may not be able to climb again," said Cristo. "My arm and shoulder are pretty bad."

"Do you care?" asked Danny, not looking at him.

Cristo looked amazed. "Of course I mind! Do you think I want to stop climbing because of one little accident?"

Danny looked down. Cristo didn't understand. The only thing Cristo could remember was coming back in the helicopter. Danny could remember it all. Danny had thought he was going to die – that they were both going to die.

"And you did a free solo round 'The Nose'. You'll be a legend at school next year," said Cristo. "Maybe you could help me do some free solo."

"No," said Danny. "I won't show you how to free solo. Your life is worth more than taking stupid risks – and so is mine. I'll never free solo again."

Cristo looked moody and hurt.

Danny stood up. "Thanks for the coke," he said.

There are some things you can't say to a friend.

Snow Dogs

by
Jane A. C. West

Zeb wants to win the dog sled race. But
will he die before he gets
to the end?

You can order *Snow Dogs* from our website at
www.barringtonstoke.co.uk

Flash Flood

by
Andy Croft

Jaz and Toni are trapped and the water is rising ... Can they make it out in time?

You can order *Flash Flood* from our website at www.barringtonstoke.co.uk

United, Here I Come!

by
Alan Combes

Joey and Jimmy are very bad at football.
But Jimmy is sure he will play for United
one day. Is Jimmy crazy?

You can order *United, Here I Come!* from our website at
www.barringtonstoke.co.uk

Help!

by
Alison Prince

Dad wants Ben's help.
He needs to fix a shower. But what
happens if Dad gets it wrong?

You can order *Help!* from our website at
www.barringtonstoke.co.uk

Thin Ice

by
Chris Powling

Pete knows that you must not walk on ice.
But a dog is stuck out there on the lake!
Pete has to help ... what can he do?

You can order *Thin Ice* from our website at
www.barringtonstoke.co.uk